THE LONELY GIANT

In memory of my mum Jane
and for my family
Jon, Henry and Millie.

First published 2016 by Walker Books Ltd,
87 Vauxhall Walk, London SE11 5HJ • 10 9 8 7 6 5 4 3 2 1
© 2016 Sophie Ambrose • The right of Sophie Ambrose to be identified as
author/illustrator of this work has been asserted by her in accordance with the
Copyright, Designs and Patents Act 1988 • This book has been typeset in Clarendon T
Printed in China • All rights reserved. No part of this book may be reproduced, transmitted or stored in an information retrieval system in any form or by
any means, graphic, electronic or mechanical, including photocopying, taping and recording, without prior written permission from the publisher. British
Library Cataloguing in Publication Data: a catalogue record for this book is available from the British Library • ISBN 978-1-4063-6154-4 • www.walker.co.uk

THE LONELY GIANT

SOPHIE AMBROSE

WALKER BOOKS
AND SUBSIDIARIES
LONDON · BOSTON · SYDNEY · AUCKLAND

In a cave, on top of a crag, in the middle of a huge forest, lived a giant. The giant spent all day, day after day, doing what giants do...

Pulling up trees as though they were weeds,

heaving and hurling huge logs like spears ...

and smashing
and mashing
mountains.

Over the years,

smaller and

and quieter and

all the birds and the animals were scared away

the forest became ...

smaller ...

quieter until ...

and the songs of the forest had gone.

At night, the giant sat alone in his cold cave.
"How quiet everything is," he sighed.
"I remember the forest full of birdsong
with plenty of wood for my fire."

The giant grew lonelier and lonelier.

Then one day when the giant was hard at work bashing and smashing, little yellow bird appeared.

She followed the giant all day long,
singing to him.

The giant enjoyed the singing so much, he caught
little yellow bird and put her in a cage.

"Now you can sing to me whenever I want," he said.
"I won't be lonely any more."

But little yellow bird grew sad ...

and the sadder she got, the less she sang.

Soon little yellow bird was too sad to sing at all.

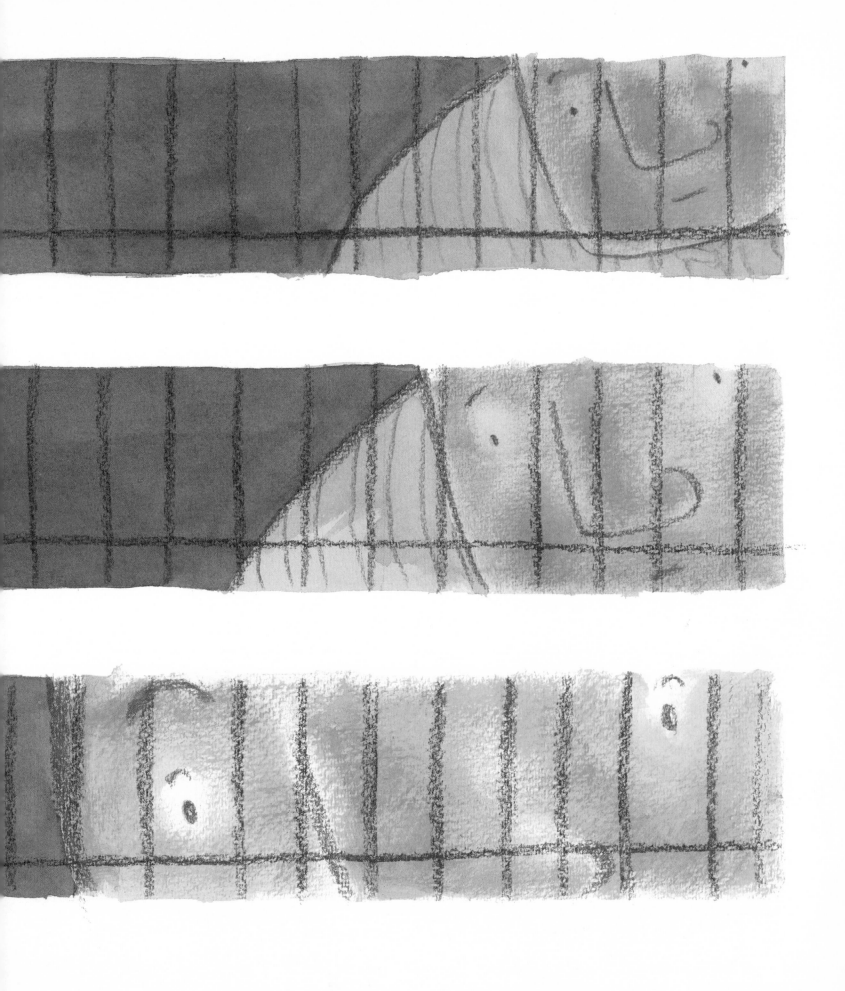

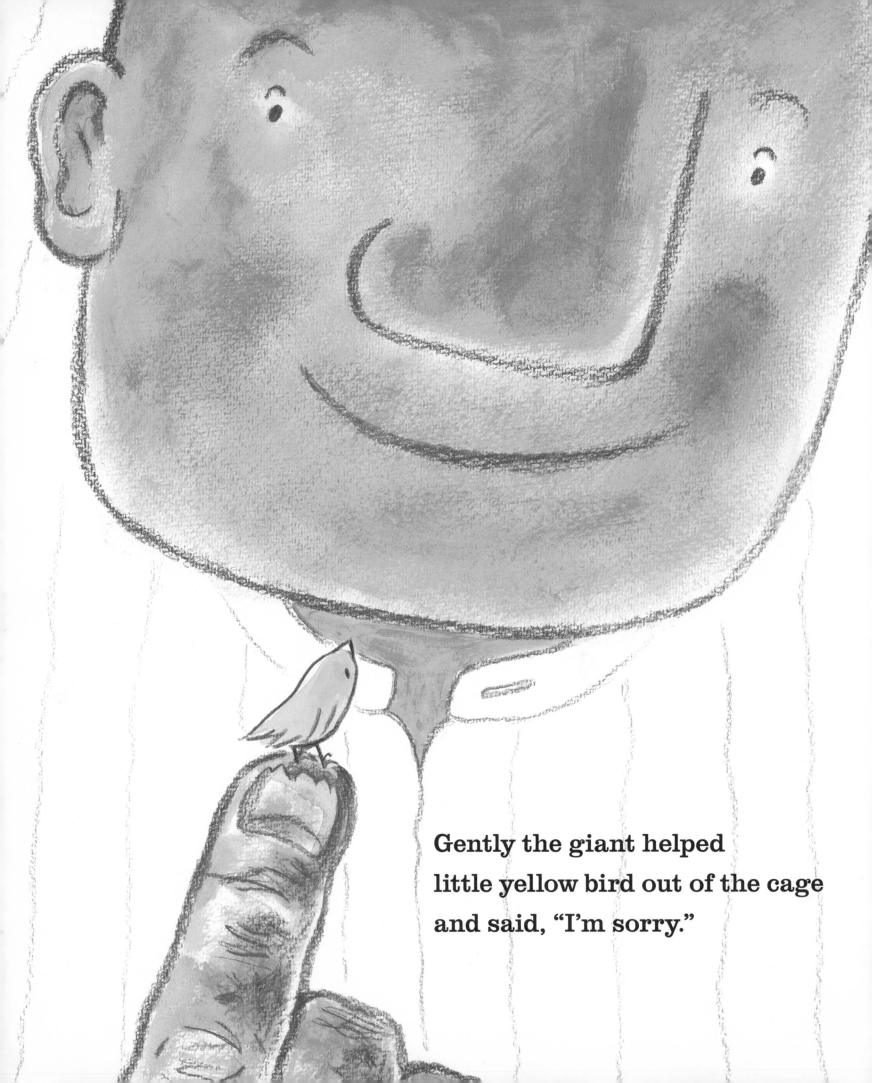

Gently the giant helped
little yellow bird out of the cage
and said, "I'm sorry."

The next morning,
when the giant looked
for little yellow bird,
she had gone.

That day the giant walked and walked looking for
little yellow bird. But there were no birds,
or trees or plants to be seen.

"If only I could bring them all back," he said.
"I must mend what I've broken."

The giant worked hard to rebuild the forest.

He sowed seeds ...

he mended mountains ...

and he planted trees.

Then the giant watched and he waited.

Slowly, over the years,

bigger and

and noisier and

all the birds and the animals came back

the forest became ...

bigger ...

noisier until ...

to their beautiful green home.

And the forest blossomed
with new life again!

The giant wasn't lonely any more.
He was happy at last.

So was little yellow bird,
whose song filled the forest all day,
every day.